THE PRIVATE CLUB

BOOK ONE

J.S. COOPER & HELEN COOPER

This book is a work of fiction. Names, characters, places, and incidents either are the product of the author's imagination or are used fictitiously. Any resemblance to actual persons, living or dead, events, or locales is entirely coincidental.

CHAPTER ONE

Nerves raced in my stomach as I made my way to the interview. The sky was grey and it was drizzling slightly. A flash of lightning cracked the sky, followed by loud, ominous thunder. I swallowed hard as I made my way along the sidewalk, walking as quickly as I could in my stripper heels. Heels I would never have worn to my job at the law firm, but then this wasn't a lawyer position.

I walked quickly into the building. I didn't want to give myself time to change my mind and hobble back home like a nervous Nellie. The building surprised me as I looked around. It was unassuming and normal. There was nothing ostentatious about it. Nothing that screamed of money or class. There was nothing that screamed 'private club' about it at all.

"Are you here about the position?" An older lady looked me over in my short, tight dress and pointed me towards a door. "Go in there. He's waiting for you."

"He?" I looked at her uncertainly. "Can you tell me his name, please? I don't want to go into the interview without knowing it." I gave her a small smile.

With narrowed eyes, she looked at me like I was crazy. "You don't need to know his name. Just go and wait in there. He'll come and get you." She looked back down at her desk and started typing on her computer. I guessed that was my dismissal, and I walked quickly to the door she had pointed me towards.

I sat there waiting in the dark hallway, playing with my long red wig, wondering what the hell I was doing. I knew nothing about bartending, and frankly, I didn't really even care to learn. I was still in shock that I'd been fired from my associate position at the law firm I'd worked so hard and tediously for. This was not a part of my life plan. I was supposed to be on a partner track, not a drinking-for-free track. I bit my lower lip as I tried to stop myself from laughing hysterically. I didn't even know if I would be allowed to drink for free as a bartender. I jumped up, ready to leave, when a door opened.

"You here for the interview?" The voice was dark and mysterious. I looked up to see the man's face, but it was hidden in the shadows. I shivered slightly as the cold air ran over my skin.

"Um, yes," I managed to squeak out and walked towards the door.

"What's your name?" he asked in a voice that was close to a growl.

"Jada." I paused right in front of him and looked up slowly. "My name's Jada." I swallowed hard as I lied. I stared at the man in front of me. He was about six foot four, with dark blue eyes and dark blond hair. I stared at his muscles through his tailored white shirt. The crisp white of his shirt complemented his golden tan and his perfect white teeth. "What's your name?" I gave him a small smile and waited for his answer. He stared at me blankly for a few seconds and then turned around and walked back into the office. I stood there uncertainly, not knowing what to do.

"Are you coming?" He looked back at me and I hurried in after him.

"Sorry, I didn't know," I mumbled and wanted to slap myself. *You are a strong, smart, independent woman, Meg O'Riley*, I lectured myself. *You are a lawyer. Do not act like a punk.*

"You didn't know what?" He raised an eyebrow at me, and I felt my face flushing.

"Nothing." I shook my head. "I'm just here for the bartending interview."

"Bartending?" He stared at me for a second and laughed. His gaze fell down to my partially exposed chest and the long expanse of my legs. "Sure."

"I am," I protested too loudly. I stared at him again for a second. Something felt slightly off in this whole situation.

"Take your clothes off." He sat down and started playing with some papers on his desk.

"What?" My voice was loud as my mouth fell open.

"I said, take your clothes off." He looked back up at me. "Now."

"I heard you." This time my voice was firm. "What you heard wasn't me asking you to repeat yourself, but more a vocal expression of my shock and anger."

"Shock and anger." He cocked his head and really looked at me then. His eyes studied my face and narrowed. "You're not really here for a bartending gig, are you?"

"That's what the advertisement said."

"Hold on." He picked his suddenly ringing phone up, but his eyes never left mine as he spoke. "This is Greyson Twining."

I watched his lips as he spoke. *Greyson. Nice name. He doesn't look like a Greyson. He looks more like a Brody or a Josh.* I looked around the room and started shivering as I realized he was still staring at me body. I knew that I should just run out of the building and leave, but my feet wouldn't move.

"I don't know what you're talking about, Brandon. You can't tell me who I can and can't hire." Greyson's voice was harsh. "No cute blondes named Meg have come in today. I gotta go." He hung up the phone and stood up again, walking over to me slowly. "So, Jada, tell me more about yourself."

He stopped in front of me and leaned in towards me. I froze as his lips stopped a mere inch from mine. I didn't know whether I should slap him across the face or close my eyes and wait for his kiss. For some reason, my body went with the latter, and I waited in sweet anticipation to feel his lips upon mine.

"So, Meg," Greyson whispered in my ear lightly. "Tell me why Brandon Hastings just called me and told me not to hire you."

My eyes opened slowly and I swallowed hard as I saw my wig in his hands. I looked into his eyes and saw that he was laughing at me. I knew I should turn away. Brandon had warned me not to come here and had called Greyson and told him not to hire me. I knew that there had to be a reason. I looked at the door and debated with myself for about ten seconds.

"I think the more important question is do I have the job." I ran my hands through my blond hair and shook it out. "Don't you think?"

"Why did you lie about your name, Meg?" He looked at me curiously.

"Why didn't you tell me your name?" I raised an eyebrow at him, my brain working furiously. "What's really going on here?"

"Do you think that's a smart question?" His eyes darkened at me. "How do you know Brandon Hastings?"

"I don't. I met him once."

"And he wanted you and you turned him down?" He smiled wide. "He never did take rejection well."

"How do you know him?" I changed the subject. Who cared how he thought I knew Brandon? Let him think what he wanted. I didn't have to tell him that Brandon was my best friend's ex-boyfriend—or current boyfriend. I wasn't even sure what was going on with the two of them right now.

"The job's yours if you want it." He glanced at me and turned around. "I'm not sure why I'm offering it to you, though. Every part of me is telling me not to offer it to you."

"Every part of me is telling me not to take it." My heart thudded as he turned to look at me. There was a dark glint in his eyes as he surveyed my face.

"You've got three days."

"Three days for what?"

"You have three days to prove to me that you can do this job." His eyes challenged me. "If, after three days, I don't think you're successful, then you are out."

"Most jobs have a probationary period of thirty days to three months." I frowned, my heart beating fast.

"This isn't most jobs."

"What is the job?"

"It's whatever you want it to be."

"That's not a proper answer."

"This isn't a *proper* job." His lips curled slightly and his eyes surveyed me expectantly, waiting for me to ask him to expand on the job definition.

"I'll take it," I said nonchalantly, pretending that my heart wasn't racing in fear and worry.

"Good." He nodded and then walked towards me. "Are they?"

"Are what what?" I frowned.

"Are they?" He smiled at stared into my eyes for a moment before dropping his gaze to my heaving breasts.

"That's not a question."

"Are they as juicy as they look?"

"Excuse me!" My voice rose as I blushed. "How dare you!"

"How dare I?" His baby blues twinkled at me. "I think you'll find I dare a lot."

"It's rude to talk about a lady's breasts," I muttered.

"I was talking about your lips." His fingers reached up and ran across my trembling lower lip. "They are so pink and juicy. I wondered if they tasted as sweet as they looked."

"Oh," I whispered, unable to move as he continued slowly caressing my lips. His fingers were both rough and gentle at the same time, and I could smell his salty musk close to me. It gave me a heady feeling, a feeling I'd never really experienced before. Greyson Twining was the type of man I'd learned to avoid: sexy, arrogant, mysterious, and all knowing. He was the sort of man you knew you could never really have. A man who would never give himself fully to a woman. And yet he'd already intrigued me enough to influence my decisions. My brain was screaming at me to run out of this dark, secretive building and away from this charismatic man with the open yet closed blue eyes.

"I want to taste them." He leaned towards me and I backed away quickly, tripping over my feet and crashing down to the floor. I sat there, staring up at him and his shuttered eyes, and shivered. He looked so tall and muscular standing above me. I swallowed hard, trying to ignore the voice in my brain that was screaming at me to pull him down with me to the floor.

He reached his hand down to me to help me up and I took it hesitantly. As soon as our fingers touched, I felt a shock of electricity course through me. His eyes looked at me in confusion for just one second as he pulled me up, but they quickly became guarded again.

He pulled me up and towards him and I stumbled into his arms. His hands circled my waist and he held me against him for two seconds before he leaned down. His teeth bit down on my lower lip and then I felt his lips sucking. I gasped and closed my eyes at the feel of him against me. His teeth were sharp and his lips were soft as he nibbled on my lip. He pulled away slowly and smiled at me.

"Strawberry gloss," he stated casually. "And yes, they are as juicy as they look."

"Don't kiss me." I pushed him away. "That's sexual harassment."

"Honey, that wasn't a kiss." He chuckled and licked his lips. "And trust me, you'll know when it's sexual."

"I don't want to know," I lied, trying to hide the fact that my body was involuntarily trembling at the thought of knowing him on a deeper, more intimate level. I was ashamed of myself for wanting this man I didn't even know. I'd never had such a base reaction to a man before. Greyson Twining intrigued me and attracted me. My loins ached to touch and be touched by him. The visceral reaction I had when I saw him made my blood boil over with heat.

"Liar."

"If you really think I'm a liar, then you shouldn't hire me."

"I don't think I should hire you. You're trouble. With a capital T." His eyes darkened and his face stilled as he gazed at me thoughtfully.

A question suddenly struck me and I spoke my thought aloud. "How do you know Brandon?"

He laughed bitterly. "I'm not sure you want to know."

"I want to know." My heart raced in fear, and this time it wasn't due to how he was making me feel. "Is he your friend?"

He shook his head. "I don't do friends."

"Is he your enemy, then?" I shivered to myself, remembering Brandon's face when he had warned me not to come to this job interview. "You don't like each other?"

"Like and dislike have nothing to do with it."

"Then what?" I frowned. "How do you know him? Tell me!" I begged.

"Why should I tell you? Who do you think you are?" He frowned back at me. "Don't forget your place, Meg. You work for me. Not the other way around."

"I wasn't trying to boss you around," I protested, frustrated. I wanted to shake him and then myself. "I'm going to go now."

"You can't leave." He shook his head. "Not if you want to pass probation."

"Then I have to call my roommate."

"You have a boyfriend?" His eyes glared at me.

"No." I looked at him curiously. "Why?"

"I wasn't sure if roommate was a code word for a boyfriend."

"It's not."

"Don't sleep with any members of the club." His eyes bored into mine. "No matter how much money they offer you."

"I wasn't planning on it."

"I'll call Patsy. She'll show you to your room."

"Okay," I said weakly, staring into his once-again distant blue eyes. I knew that he was dismissing me, but I didn't know what else to say. I couldn't really ask him to let me stay and chat with him. How pathetic would I sound if I said that I didn't want to leave his company just yet?

"Patsy, it's Greyson. We have a new girl. She's in my office. Come and get her, please." His voice was gruff as he spoke into the phone and sat back down again. "You can go back into the hallway and wait. She'll be along to collect you in a minute."

"Okay." I turned away, feeling embarrassed and rejected. *Get a grip, Meg. You're way too smart and secure for these teenage-girl feelings.* It had been a long time since I had such an immediate reaction to a guy.

"Oh, and Meg—I'd be careful about letting people you know Brandon Hastings." His voice was quiet. "There are some folks around here that knew him quite well, and let's just say that if they knew you were well acquainted with him, you could find your time here fairly contentious."

I walked through the door without responding or looking back. My heart was beating rapidly, and all I wanted to do was run away and never come back. I didn't like Greyson and I didn't like this club. If I were honest, my curiosity was piqued about the club and the job, but a part of me didn't really want to know. My entire body was screaming at me to run like wildfire. But I didn't. I needed to find out what Brandon's involvement with the club had been. I needed to find out the truth for Katie before she fully committed to him. Every fiber of my being told me that Greyson Twining was bad news, and I was now worried that Brandon Hastings was even worse.

I sat there for a few seconds before I started growing angry. I jumped up and went back into his office. Greyson looked up at me with a surprised frown, and I could see from his expression that he was angry.

"What are you doing in here?" His words were dismissive and he looked toward the open door. "I told you to go and wait outside."

"I know what you said." I glared at him and walked towards his desk. "I just wanted to tell you that I expect you to not violate my space again. I don't want you touching me or kissing me or doing anything to me. Do you understand?" The words spewed out of my mouth quickly and I stared at him anxiously, expecting him to be angry. I was surprised to see his eyes glittering and his lips twitching. "Do you understand?" I asked again, glaring at him.

"I understand." He nodded. I stood there tensely, waiting for the ball to drop and for Greyson to stand up and push me against the wall and put me in my place. I was tingling, waiting in sweet anticipation for him to try to overpower me. I could picture myself slapping him and pushing him away.

"Anything else?" He held his pen in the air and stared at me expectantly.

"No." I shook my head, disappointed that I wasn't going to get the showdown that I wanted.

"Okay, then you can go back out and wait for Patsy." His voice was dismissive, and I felt even worse than I had before. I turned around slowly and walked back to the door, feeling like an idiot.

"Oh, and Meg." His voice was deceptively soft behind me. I paused to listen but didn't turn back around to face him. "I'm going to honor your wishes. The next time my lips meet yours will be because you begged me to kiss you. It will be because you couldn't go another second without the feel of my hands caressing your body." He paused for a second, and I remained where I was, standing to see if he was going to say anything else. "And when you beg me to take you, hard and fast,

I won't say no. In fact, I'll pound you so hard that you'll wonder where your body ends and mine begins."

I swallowed hard, and it took everything in me to not turn around and face him. I waited for a few more seconds but silence filled the air. I quickly exited the room and closed the door behind me. I leaned back and closed my eyes, but all I could see in my mind was Greyson. Tall, dominant, elusive Greyson. It was at that moment that I knew I was in trouble.

CHAPTER TWO

"What's your name?" Her voice was disinterested as she looked me over.

"Meg." I tried smiling at her.

"Starla." She flipped her long, raven-black hair and opened a door.

"Nice to meet you, Starla."

"No, you're going to go by Starla. Meg's too plain, too girl-next-door. Men don't want a Meg. You're Starla from now on."

"Oh." I paused and debated whether or not I should say something. I was still annoyed and frustrated at Greyson's dismissal, and I didn't appreciate her condescending tone.

"And if you're sticking with blond, you should think about tanning. You look washed out. If you want to stick with the pale look, I suggest you go strawberry red. And then maybe you can keep Meg."

"I'm a natural blonde."

"Sure, doll." She ushered me into the small, dark room. "This is your room. You'll be sharing it with the other new girl. She's not here yet."

"Sharing?"

"Yeah, sharing. This is a trial period. If Greyson likes you, you'll get your own room. For now, you get to choose a bunk."

"I don't need a room, I have my own apartment." I looked around the room distastefully.

"Then why are you here?"

"For a job." I sighed and looked away from her gaze. I felt out of place and even more uncomfortable than before. "I needed a job."

"And the club is the first place you thought to look?"

"I thought it would be easy money to bartend and allow me to look for another law position in the daytime."

"Law?"

"I'm a lawyer."

"Oh, fancy-schmancy." She laughed bitterly. "Now you're just one of the girls, Starla."

"I'm Meg," I whispered, but I don't think she heard me. "Does the training start tomorrow?"

"Training?" she frowned.

"I don't have much experience bartending."

"I wouldn't worry about that!" She burst out laughing and looked me over. "It seems to me you have the requisite skills for the job." She stared at my scantily-covered breasts and nodded. "I guess all your lawyer skills are going to come in handy."

"What does that mean?" My voice rose.

"What?" Her eyes narrowed and she looked at me in surprise.

"Your comment means what?" I gave her a sharp look. "Look, I don't know you and you don't know me, so I'm going to assume that you're not being a bitch on purpose. Maybe you just had a bad day?" I took a deep breath and was about to continue when I watched the expression on her face change.

"You're not as pathetic as you look, are you?" She smiled, and I could see a new respect in her eyes.

"I don't look—"

"No need to get riled up, Starla," she laughed. "Day one hasn't even started yet."

"I'm not riled up," I shot back, annoyed.

"I'm surprised Greyson chose you. He usually prefers the submissive girls."

"I'm not submissive."

"No, you're not." She looked at me appraisingly. "I'm not even sure why you're here."

"I told you why I'm here. I needed a job."

"Yeah, yeah." Her eyes grew cloudy, and I could tell she was thinking. "I know why you came. I just don't know why Greyson let you stay."

"What do you mean?" I frowned, my heart pounding. Talking about Greyson was heating me up even more.

"Nothing." She shook her head, and this time she looked me over again carefully. "I just hope he knows what he's doing."

"Will he be there tomorrow?" I tried to ask casually, but my ears were perked up, eagerly waiting for her answer.

"Greyson?" She gave me a look. "Not at all. Greyson has nothing to do with the girls. I doubt you'll see him again for the rest of the week."

"Oh, okay." I felt a surge of disappointment at her words. I tried to tell myself that it was due to the fact that I wasn't going to be able to get much information about Brandon without seeing him. My body was calling me a liar, though.

"Just relax and wait for the next girl." She walked to the door and stopped before she left. "By the way, I'm Raven. I'll be helping you this week."

"I thought you were Patsy?" I frowned and she laughed.

"Do you think men prefer an exotic dark-haired beauty called Raven or a mousy brunette called Patsy?" She raised an eyebrow at me and then walked out of the room, leaving me standing there wondering what the hell I had gotten myself into.

I was surprised by Patsy's appearance. While she was beautiful, she was older than I thought she would be. She had to have been in her late thirties, though she hid it well. I wanted to call after her and ask her more questions, but for some reason I didn't trust that the answers she would provide would be true.

***

A few hours later, the door opened slowly and my breath caught as I waited to see who was going to walk thought the door. My heart skipped a beat and my fingers quickly smoothed down my hair as I waited for Greyson to walk through the door.

"Hello," a young voice squeaked and I looked up in surprise and disappointment.

"Hi."

"I'm Nancy." She walked into the room and I was able to see her properly now. I frowned as I stared at her. If I thought Patsy had looked too old to be working here, then Nancy looked too young. She couldn't have been older than eighteen.

"Meg," I said and smiled at her warmly. "Or, I guess, Starla now."

"Meg or Starla?" She gave me a wry smile.

"That's the name Patsy said I should use." I shrugged.

"Oh, she told me to use Pippi." The girl smiled. "There's no way in hell I'm telling anyone my name is Pippi."

"That's how I feel about Starla." I laughed and she joined in. She looked different when she laughed. I studied her face again to see who my new roommate was going to be. She reminded me of Katie in a way, from back when we had started college. Her long brown hair shone like silk and her big brown eyes were open and wide, showing all of her emotions. In this very moment, I could tell that she was excited, scared, and slightly worried. She felt the exact same way I did, and that gave me comfort. "So did you just get a job here as well?" I asked, wanting to continue the conversation. Instinctively, I trusted Nancy, and I wanted to find out what she knew.

"Yeah." She nodded and she looked away from me. "I did."

"Not happy about it?" I jumped off of the bed and walked over to her.

"No, I'm very happy. I wanted this job." She looked up at me. "I needed this job."

"Can I ask you something?" I bit my lip, and she nodded apprehensively. "Do you know what this job is, exactly? I'm not really sure, and no one will tell me."

"Oh." Her eyes looked at me in shock, and I could tell that she was surprised by my question. "You don't know?"

"No," I sighed. "I applied for a job as a bartender, and I'm not sure that what I'm going to be doing is bartending. I know, I know. I should have run out of here as soon as I sensed something was up, but my best friend's boyfriend—well, ex-boyfriend—told me not to take it and I just found out that he may be involved with the club somehow and ..." My voice trailed off as I realized how much I was babbling. "Sorry, I didn't mean to overwhelm you. I guess I needed to get that off of my chest."

"My sister disappeared." Nancy's voice was soft, and I could see unshed tears in her eyes. I froze at her words and stared at her. "My sister got a job here about ten years ago. She was really excited. My parents and I didn't really know what was going on. But she never came back."

"What do you mean she never came back?" My mind went into lawyer overload. I'd always enjoyed criminal law in law school, and part of me had always wanted to be a detective.

"I'm not really sure what happened." She shook her head. "I was only nine when my sister left. My parents were upset with Maria. They wanted her to go to college, but instead she started working at some private club and started dating some older man. We never really got to meet him, but I saw her with him once." Her eyes glazed over. "Then she just disappeared. I thought my parents had disowned her, but my dad passed away last year and my mother told me that they never knew what happened to her."

"What?"

"I know. I can't believe my dad never tried to find her." Tears started falling from Nancy's eyes and raced each other down her face. "So I've decided to try and find her. And this is where I start. This is my only clue." She bit her lower lip, and I could see her fingers trembling as she gestured around the room. "She got a job here, and I'm pretty sure the guy she was dating was from the club."

"A patron?"

"I don't know." She shrugged. "He could have worked here as well."

"I guess you'll know him when you see him."

"I don't know." She shook her head. "I only saw the back of him."

"Oh."

"And to answer your question, I have absolutely no idea what our jobs will entail."

"I'm a bit scared."

"So am I." Her face was white. "So am I."

***

The sunrise woke me up early the next morning. I lay in the top bunk listening to Nancy snoring and stared through the window. The sky was a light orange, and I could see the gardens through the glass. I ran my hands through my hair and thought about Katie and Brandon, wondering how they were getting on.

Katie had been my best friend for a long time, and I had witnessed how Brandon had torn her apart when he had dumped her in college. I had felt helpless in comforting her and slightly envious that Katie had already experienced a great love, whereas I had barely experienced a soggy kiss.

Men and I never seemed to mesh. The men I liked never really liked me, and the men I didn't like loved me in droves. I'd had a couple of relationships with suitable men, but I'd always found them to be a bit boring. I was boring, so I didn't want to date boring men. I wanted a man who was handsome and sexy and dangerous. A man who could make me melt with a glance. A man like Greyson.

I closed my eyes and allowed myself to think about Greyson. He ticked off every box on my list, but he came with a couple of disclaimers I wasn't quite sure about: heartbreaker and illegal.

"Are you awake, Meg?" Nancy whispered to me softly and I smiled. I was really lucky that I had gotten paired with Nancy.

"Yeah, I am."

"What do you think we're going to do today?"

"I have no idea."

"It's such a weird concept. I wonder if my sister had to go through this."

"Who knows?"

"Will you help me?" She spoke slowly and my fingers froze in my hair.

"Find out about your sister?"

"Yeah." She got out of her bed and stood up so that her face was close to mine in the top bunk. "You're a lawyer and you're already investigating stuff for your best friend. I was thinking maybe you could help me as well."

"I suppose." The words tripped out of my mouth before I had time to say no. I was already regretting telling her that I thought my best friend was dating a guy who had a connection to the club.

"Oh my God, really?" Nancy's eyes widened with happiness. "Oh my God, that would mean so much."

"I don't know that I could really help much."

"Oh, you would be a godsend." Nancy's fingers gripped my sheets. "I honestly have no idea what to do next."

"You got this job. You know enough." I sat up, rolled my legs over the edge of the bed, and then started laughing hysterically as I stared at Nancy's eager face.

"Are you okay?" She gave me a worried expression.

"I feel like I'm in college again." My words sounded bemused. "You remind me of my best friend, Katie. We were roommates for most of college. And I was always there as her sounding board."

"You don't sound happy about that." Nancy's voice was soft, and I stared at her in surprise.

"You know, I've never really thought about it before. But you're right. It got old being her sounding board. You're pretty astute."

"It's hard, isn't it? Being number two."

"Number two?" I frowned and rubbed the sleep from my eyes.

"I'm guessing if you were the sounding board in the friendship, she was the one who had the boys and the fun." Nancy looked at me with a question in her eyes.

"I guess so. Though I never looked at it like that before. It was more like she had all these experiences and I just felt like the one who got left behind. Like all I wanted from life was to be a lawyer or travel the world."

"Yeah, I'm the smart one." Nancy shrugged. "Maria was the beautiful one. My parents always used to thank God that I got the brains and she got the looks."

"But you're beautiful."

"Not when compared to my sister." She smiled at me softly. "Maria was the kind of beauty that could sink ships. My dad used to say they should have named her Helen."

"Helen?"

"Like Helen of Troy."

"Oh."

"Yeah, my dad is ..." she paused, "or rather, *was* a very funny man."

"I'm sorry he passed away."

"It's okay. My mom warned him about the food he used to eat." She shrugged and looked down. "He had a heart attack. My mom blames the steaks. I blame my sister."

"Your sister?"

"He was never the same after she left." She looked back up at me. "I think she broke his heart."

"I don't understand why he didn't look for her."

"She got engaged." Nancy sighed. "They all had an argument. My dad thought she chose the fiancé over her family. Well, I don't think she did."

"Whoa, what?" I jumped down from the bed. "What do you think happened?"

"Well, the guy she was dating, he seemed to—"

BANG BANG.

Nancy and I both jumped as we heard the loud knocks on the door.

"Hello?" I called out timidly and shook my head at myself. Since when had I become scared of a few loud knocks?

"Are you girls up?" Patsy's voice called through the door.

"Yes," I called back and watched as she walked in. She looked her age this morning. She had no makeup on and her hair was in rollers. She was also wearing a t-shirt and sweatpants and looked very unglamorous. She grinned as she stared at Nancy and me and the shock in our faces. "We all look normal at some point in the day."

"You look very beautiful," Nancy squeaked out and I nodded.

"Don't lie, girls." She looked us over. "You both need to get ready so you can meet the other new recruits and some of the staff."

"Do we learn about the positions today then?" I spoke up, curious as to when we were going to find out what our actual jobs were to be.

"Unlikely."

"Will we see Greyson? I mean, Mr. Twining?"

"No, he doesn't have much to do with the girls." She shook her head and frowned at me. "Mr. Twining is the owner of the club. He has much more important things to deal with."

"I understand." I blushed, feeling embarrassed.

"Will I get to meet him?" Nancy spoke up, and I could tell that she was wondering if Greyson was the man her sister had dated. In fact, I was starting to wonder that myself.

"If you make it past the three days." Patsy turned around. "Now, go shower and get ready. We have a long day ahead of us." She strolled out of the room. "Meet me in the courtyard in an hour. You'll see the other girls there as well."

"Okay." I nodded, and Nancy sat on her bed. "I wonder how many other girls are here." I looked at Nancy and she shrugged.

"Who knows?" She jumped up. "I'm going to go shower. Coming?"

"No." I shook my head. "I'm going to have a quick look around first."

"Wow." Her eyes widened. "Really?"

"Really!" I laughed. "I want to figure out where I am and what's going on."

"You're brave."

"Aren't you here to figure out what happened to your sister?"

"Yeah, but I'm going to build up to it. What if you see Greyson? Won't you be scared?"

"No." My heart beat fast and I looked away.

"I'd be so scared to see him. He's so handsome and strong. He makes my legs shake."

"Yeah, he is a bit intimidating." I gave her a weak smile.

"Good luck, Meg. I could never do what you're doing."

"Then I guess you're lucky you'll have my help." I smiled. "Let me go now, before I chicken out."

"See ya, Meg."

"Thanks." I gave her a quick smile and hurried out of the room, my brain turning everything over. Something didn't seem right, and I wasn't sure what had my brain whirling.

I hurried down the cold hallway and quickly turned the corner. I paused as I saw two men talking hurriedly at the other end of the corridor. I walked quickly to a door and pushed it open so I could hide. For some reason, I knew that it would be a mistake to let the two men see me. I leaned against the door and tried to control my breathing. And then it hit me.

Nancy had said that she'd be scared to see Greyson because he was so handsome and strong. But how did she know? From all accounts she had never met Greyson before. She'd even asked Patsy if she would get to meet him. It didn't make sense that she would ask about meeting him if she had already met him.

Why would she lie? She had either lied to me or to Patsy. Did she know more about her sister's boyfriend than she was letting on? I rubbed my forehead and looked around the room curiously.

I was in what appeared to be a child's nursery. There were cribs and toys, and I shivered at how creepy it was. Everything about this setup was creepy, and I wanted out. I was no Poirot, and at this moment I didn't want to be one.

I opened the door slowly and paused as the two men walked past the door, still talking.

"If she figures it out, Greyson and Brandon will be destroyed."

"Maybe we should help her figure it out then." The other guy laughed. I peeked through the door to see if I could catch a glimpse of their faces, but their backs were now to me.

"If the truth gets out …" One of the guys stopped. "This place will blow up."

"When you play with fire …" the other guy started, and they both laughed.

"What if he finds out first?"

"Then she's gone."

"Like the others."

"Yeah."

"We gotta do what we gotta do."

They rounded the corner then, and I stood there, rooted to the spot. I should find the exit and run. I should leave and never come back. I should go and call Katie and tell her that I thought Brandon was bad news. Very bad news. But I didn't. I exited the door and walked back quickly to my room. I hurried into my safe haven and then stopped as I saw who was in the room.

"Good morning, Meg." His voice was as deep as I remembered it being.

"Greyson." I nodded, my face flushing red as my eyes stared at him eagerly. He looked like a golden god, all toned and muscular. The tips of his hair were damp, and I realized that he must have just come out of the shower.

"How was your night?" His tone was monotone, but his eyes surveyed me with more interest.

"Good."

"Good." He smiled. "Ready for day one?"

"I guess."

"Don't sound so eager."

"Why are you here?"

"Because I own this building and the club?" He shrugged nonchalantly.

"Why are you in this room?" I tried to ignore the stirring in my stomach as I felt his blue eyes staring at my bare legs.

"I came to see you."

"Why?"

"Because I was passing the room and I wanted to say good morning."

"I see."

"Where were you?" He frowned and walked over to me. His fingers ran down my hair and he bent his nose to my neck and sniffed. "You weren't in the shower."

"Are you saying I smell?" I glared up at him and ignored the want to run my fingers across his jaw.

"I'm saying you don't smell like soap." His lips curled up. "And your hair isn't wet, which it would be if you had just been in the shower."

"Your hair is wet," I mumbled as I stared at his glistening locks.

"I can take another shower if you want."

"Why would I want that?"

"If you need a shower buddy. Someone to wash your back." His eyes twinkled as his fingers ran down my back. "I don't mind getting wet again."

"That's okay. Thanks." I took a step back and he took a step forward.

"Don't you like getting wet, Meg?" He took another step towards me, and I stepped back into the door. He placed an arm above my shoulder and pinned me back against the wall. "I'd love to see you wet."

I blinked up at him, trying to ignore the heat that was rising up through me. I adjusted my legs.

He laughed before bending his lips to my ear. "It seems like you're already a little wet."

"You're an obnoxious ass." I pushed against his chest, but he remained rigid.

"Do you really think so?" His breath was warm in my ear and I closed my eyes.

My body trembled as I felt him push himself against me harder. My nostrils expanded in ecstasy as I took in his scent and felt his warmth against me, warming me up.

"Yes," I whispered, shivering slightly as I saw the undisguised lust in his eyes. "I thought I told you I didn't want you to touch me."

"You lied."

"No, I didn't."

"Your lips are lying, but the rest of your body isn't," he whispered against my lips. "You want me to kiss you now."

"No, I don't." I shook my head, my eyes wide. "In fact, I've decided I'm leaving the program. I don't want to work here anymore."

"What?" He took a step back then and his eyes looked disappointed. "What do you mean?"

"I don't want to work here, and I don't want to put up with you."

"Liar." He looked at me angrily. "Did you speak to Brandon?"

"No."

"Come and have breakfast with me."

"No. I'm supposed to meet Patsy and the other girls in about thirty minutes in the courtyard."

"So you're staying then?" He cocked his head and stared at me through hard eyes.

"No. But I'm going to go and tell Patsy that I'm leaving."

"I knew you wouldn't make it." He turned away from me.

"Excuse me?"

"Girls like you can't handle a place like this or a man like me."

"A man like you?" My eyes widened at his words.

"I was going to train you." He looked at me again.

"I thought you didn't interact with the girls." I frowned, remembering Patsy's words.

"I do. In special cases."

"I'm a special case?"

"You could be."

"Why did you come to my room, Greyson?"

"Where were you if you didn't go in the shower?"

"You better leave before my roommate comes back." I licked my lower lip, and Greyson and I stared at each other for about a minute without saying a word.

"What is it about you, Meg?"

"What do you mean?"

"Nothing." He shook his head and ran his hand through his hair. "Don't leave."

"Why not?"

"I don't want you to go."

"You don't even know me." I frowned, and for one brief moment I thought that he was going to say something romantic and sweet. I could fully admit that I was a hopeless romantic, and I waited with bated breath for him to tell me something along the lines of "I've known you all my life, Meg."

"I want to make love to you." His words were rough, and I swallowed hard as he grabbed my hand and brought it to his erection. "You did this to me."

"You're crude." I pulled my hand away from his hardness and looked up at him in distaste. "This is why I'm leaving."

"Because you turn me on?"

"No, because you think it's acceptable to grab my hand and put it there."

"Put it where?" He smiled evilly.

"You know where."

"Say it."

"Against you."

"Against me?"

"Against your hardness!" I muttered, irritated.

"Against my rigid, tormented, hard cock, you mean." He grinned at me. Then his hands grabbed my waist and pulled me against him. "Don't be scared to say the words."

"I'm not scared."

"Can I kiss you?" He looked down at me and I shook my head. "Please?" His hands grabbed my ass and squeezed. I swallowed hard and shook my head again.

My brain was buzzing with lust and confusion. I could barely form a coherent thought as he held me against him. *This is what sexual tension feels like*, I thought to myself. I'd never felt this way about a man before. Never. Not even the men I had dated for months. Let alone for a man I'd barely known twenty-four hours.

"Will you kiss me, then?" His tongue traced the lines of my lips as he whispered against them.

"No," I squeaked out. I gasped as I felt his tongue touch mine for one quick second before he pulled back. "You should leave."

"If that's what you want." His lips pulled back slightly, and I felt disappointed.

"That's what I want." I nodded and my body stood still as his fingers continued massaging my butt cheeks.

"Then I'll go." He nodded down at me, but he didn't move. His fingers slipped between my legs and I felt them brush against my private spot lightly before he stepped back. "Have a good morning, Meg." He gave me a quick smile and walked to the door.

I listened to the door open and close, and I stood there with my eyes closed, replaying the scene in my mind. My panties felt wet and my whole body was throbbing in anticipation. He'd barely touched me. I could have blinked and missed the light touch of his fingertips against me, but it was all I could think about. My nerve endings were on high alert and my mouth was screaming at me for not allowing his sweet tongue to explore its depths.

I sank back against the wall and all I wanted to do was scream. I had no idea what to do. Every fiber of my being was screaming at me to leave this place, this club. But there was a voice that was whispering in my head, telling me to stay. My body was alive and on fire in a way that it had never been before. But not only that, my brain was on high alert. There was something going on here. Something big. Something that didn't make sense. Something that could get someone hurt. Something that could get *me* hurt. But I ignored the warning bells in my head.

I'd been a doormat for too long. I wanted an adventure. I wanted to find out what this private club was all about. I wanted to find out Greyson's story. I couldn't lie to myself anymore. This was about more than helping Nancy and figuring out what was up with Brandon. I wanted Greyson Twining. Even if it meant I was going to get burned. Maybe it was time for me to play with the fire. Staying back from the flames hadn't helped me in my love life. I was ready to feel the heat.

CHAPTER THREE

Nancy and I silently walked to the courtyard. I was still out of breath from running to the bathroom to shower and then back to the room. Nancy had been waiting for me in the room when I got back, but we hadn't had time to talk since we were running behind.

"Glad you could join us, girls." Patsy's face was somber, and I knew whatever bonding we had experienced this morning was long gone. I stared at the other girls and frowned to myself. Aside from Patsy, I seemed to be the oldest one there—and by a long shot. I'd never thought I was old at twenty-five, but standing with all these girls in their late teens made me feel like I was positively ancient. I could tell that I wasn't the only one who had realized that I was the odd one out. There was another blond girl staring at me and whispering to her two sidekicks.

One of them laughed as they looked me up and down, and I tried not to roll my eyes.

"Welcome to the club, ladies." Patsy gestured for everyone to follow her. "This is day one of your three-day orientation."

The blonde who had been staring at me spoke up. "When do we meet the men?"

"If you're talking about the heads of security, you'll be meeting them today." Patsy's voice was dry, and I wondered if this was some sort of strip club. It would make sense. Maybe it was a strip club for the rich, famous, and powerful. Maybe this was the sort of club that had no rules. I shuddered at the thought of being expected to have sex with men for money.

"Are they paying customers?" the blonde said and Patsy gave her a chilling stare.

"I'm not sure what you mean by that comment. This isn't a *Girls Gone Wild* video." Patsy looked at the rest of us. "Any other impertinent questions?"

We were all silent, and I cheered inside at the jab the blonde had received. I was already feeling like the redheaded stepchild, and it was nice to see negative attention directed at someone else. I stared at the other girls again and frowned to myself. I really didn't understand why I had been chosen to move forward in the probation period. I sure didn't feel like I fit the type they were going for.

"Shall we introduce ourselves?" Patsy stopped by a beautiful water fountain, and I looked around the garden again. It reminded me of some ancient Greek setting, with its tall white columns and large expanses of grass and marble. It was grand— really grand. I felt like I was in some rich man's mansion and not in what was possibly a strip club. But I supposed I'd never seen a high-class strip club, only the seedy ones on TV. Being in this setting would make everything seem classier, even selling your body for money.

I shivered as I thought about sleeping with someone for money. There was no way in hell I was going to do that. I'd leave before that happened. I wanted to find out what was going on, but not that badly.

"I'm Elizabeth," the blonde said confidently. "I'm nineteen, from Connecticut. I'm a freshman at Dartmouth, but I'm taking a year off." She smiled. "I applied for a job here because I wanted to make some money and explore the world."

I stared at her beautiful smile in confusion. In many ways, she reminded me of myself at eighteen, only I hadn't been as confident and I certainly wouldn't have dropped out of school.

My brain tuned out as the other girls started talking. An overwhelming feeling of sadness encompassed me as I stood there. I felt like a loser. How had I ended up here? What was I doing? Had I lost my mind? I was a lawyer, for heaven's sake. I had a degree from an Ivy League university. I had an apartment in Manhattan. I was responsible, smart, in charge of my own life.

But you're bored, a voice whispered in my head. *Where has your perfectly lived life gotten you?*

I thought about Katie and the drama in her life when it came to Brandon. She loved hard and got hurt hard, but still she was living her life and trying again. She was going for it. I didn't want to be the woman who got to be eighty years old and had never had a real love or heartbreak.

"Oh, Mr. Twining." Patsy's voice sounded reverent and the garden grew instantly still as I froze. "I didn't expect to see you here today." She cleared her throat, and I looked up to see Patsy blushing. I looked to her right and there stood Greyson. He was dressed properly now in a navy suit, and I could see all the girls staring at him in admiration. I looked at Nancy's face quickly to see her expression, but it was blank. She wasn't giving anything away.

"Good morning, Patsy. Good morning, girls." He nodded and gave us all a welcoming smile. "My name is Greyson Twining. I'm one of the owners of the club."

"Hi, Greyson," Elizabeth called out and gave a little wave. Greyson gave her a huge smile back and I felt like screaming. "I'm Elizabeth."

"Nice to meet you, Elizabeth."

"I'm in the Rainbow Room if you want to stop by tonight," she continued, and the two girls next to her giggled nervously.

"That's enough." Patsy's voice was loud and angry. "I'm sorry, Mr. Twining. This is day one. They don't know all the rules yet."

"No worries." He nodded, and I felt his eyes on me. I looked up and he gave me a small smile. I didn't smile back, even though my insides were heating up. "I actually came to see how everyone was getting on before I went to a meeting."

Elizabeth spoke up again. "Will we get to meet the other owner?"

I frowned.

"No." Greyson's expression changed and he was no longer smiling. Patsy was glaring at the girl, and I could tell that the mention of the other owner was something they didn't like being mentioned.

"Oh, that's a pity. I'd quite like to meet Mr. Hastings," Elizabeth continued, and I stared at Greyson. He looked at me quickly and his eyes bored into mine with a challenge.

"That's enough, Elizabeth," Patsy said. Then she turned around and whispered something to Greyson. He looked thoughtful for a moment and then nodded. All the while, his eyes never left mine.

"What do you think, Meg?" He spoke quietly, but I could still hear an acerbic hint in his tone.

"What do I think of what?"

"Of us contacting Mr. Hastings?"

"I didn't know he was involved with the club."

"There are many things it seems you don't know."

"But I'd love to find out." I smiled at him and raised an eyebrow.

"It was nice meeting you girls." He nodded and turned to Patsy. "I'll see you later."

"Thanks for coming out, Mr. Twining. I know you are busy," Patsy beamed at him, and we all watched as he went back into the building.

"I'd fuck him in a heartbeat," Elizabeth proclaimed and her friends giggled. "He wouldn't even have to pay me."

"That's why he's the boss," another girl whispered and they all nodded.

"Girls, I'll be right back," Patsy suddenly exclaimed and walked out of the garden. I turned to Nancy.

"That was weird, wasn't it?"

"Yeah." Her eyes were buzzing with something. "I wonder if we'll get to see Greyson again."

"Do you know him?" I asked her softly, not wanting her to know how important her answer was to me.

"No, of course not." She shook her head. "That girl, Elizabeth, looks like she is going to be a bitch."

"Yeah, she doesn't look nice."

"I thought she was going to kill you when Greyson said your name."

"Oh."

"Do you know him?"

"No, I just met him yesterday for about a minute," I lied for some reason. "He seems like a nice guy."

Nancy made a face. "I don't know that I would call him nice."

"So you do know him?"

"I know of him," Nancy sighed. "I know about him and Brandon Hastings."

"Oh?"

"The guy that Elizabeth mentioned." Nancy looked around and then whispered in my ear. "He was one of the founders. Along with Greyson."

"How do you know?"

"We can't talk about it here." She shook her head. "Later."

"Okay." I nodded in agreement. What else was Nancy hiding from me?

"Good morning, girls," a deep, gruff voice shouted out, and I looked up and froze. There were three men standing at the front, all dressed in the same uniform. The uniform was instantly recognizable to me as the same outfit the two men I'd seen earlier were wearing. But I couldn't tell which two men out of the three in front of me I'd seen.

"Hi, girls. My name is David. I'm the head of security here at the club. I'd like to introduce myself and the two guys I work with, Bruno and Frank."

"Hi, guys," Elizabeth called out flirtatiously.

"We are here to make sure that your time working at the club is a safe and comfortable one," David continued in a serious voice while Frank and Bruno smiled at Elizabeth. I was pretty sure I knew who the two I'd seen in the corridor were now. "If at any time, you feel uncomfortable or in danger, you should call us immediately. Those who get through the first three days in training will be given a button that you will wear at all times. In the middle of the button, there is a small stone. Push the stone and we will be alerted right away. Each button is equipped with GPS, so we will be able to locate you as well." He looked around the group and paused. When he looked at me, I noticed a quick flash of surprise before he moved on.

I stared at him and wondered what his story was. He was a handsome man, but more in the retired-boxer kind of way. He was tall and stocky, with a buzz cut and deep blue eyes. His bulging muscles were filled with tattoos and he stood with a straight and rigid back. He reminded me of some ex-military men I'd met the summer before at the Navy pier.

I then checked out the other two guys. They both looked like boys trying to play men. They were both about my age and had average builds. One of the guys had really bad acne and his eyes looked cold. He looked like the sort of guy that would make you shiver in fear if you saw him on a dark night. I wasn't sure if he was Frank or Bruno, but I knew that I didn't want to spend any one-on-one time with him.

"Any questions?" David continued, and I realized that I had spaced out.

"When are we going to learn what our job descriptions are?" Nancy spoke, and I looked at her in surprise. I hadn't thought that she'd wanted to draw any attention to herself.

"Not until you pass the first three days," Patsy answered, and I looked around to see if Greyson had come back with her.

"When can we call our friends and family?" another girl asked, and Patsy gave her a hard look.

"So today, you girls will cycle through ten different rooms. Each of you will go in one room at a time. Each room will be testing you for a particular quality or skill. You have to complete the assignment in each room to the best of your ability."

"Oh, shit, this isn't going to be some written exam, is it?" Elizabeth moaned. "I'm taking a break from college to get away from that shit."

"Such a vocabulary for a Dartmouth girl." The words were out of my mouth before I could stop myself.

"Did you say something, Grandma?" she shot back at me, and all the other girls, except Nancy, started laughing.

"I'd rather be a grandma than a bimbo," I muttered under my breath, and Nancy squeezed my arm.

"Ladies, let's stop with the name-calling." Patsy sighed. "We are all friends here."

"Until someone becomes more popular," Nancy muttered to herself, and once again I realized that she wasn't as clueless as she had made herself to be yesterday.

***

The first room I entered was bare aside from a black leather couch and a small side table. I looked around, wondering what I was supposed to do. There was no paper, and I couldn't see any guidebooks. I stood by the door for a few minutes, waiting for someone to walk in, and then I walked over to the couch and sat down. I sat there in silence for a few more minutes, and then a voice spoke into the room. I jumped up in surprise, taken aback by the suddenness of the voice. I looked around the room, and it was then that I saw the speaker in the corner.

"Stand up," the voice commanded me, and I stood up slowly. "Do a jumping jack," it said, and I stood there for a moment feeling foolish.

"A jumping jack?" I spoke back to the voice and waited. The lights went out then and I sat back down on the couch, wondering if I had already failed the test. All of a sudden, I heard some music playing from the speakers. It sounded like some old-school R&B, something I'd listened to in grade school. The sound of the door opening made me jump again and I turned around quickly to see who had joined me in the room.

"You don't like to listen to instructions, do you?" I couldn't mistake Greyson's voice, and I felt my cheeks warming.

"What are you doing here?" I sounded anxious and weak, and I wanted to rewind the clock so I could answer him in a stronger voice.

"I came to see how you were doing." He walked towards me, his voice lower and harder to hear above the men crying out about making love to me.

"I thought you didn't have anything to do with the training." I spoke more firmly this time. I wanted him to know he didn't affect me.

"I don't." He slipped onto the couch next to me. "Not usually."

"So why are you here?" I questioned him, peering up into his face curiously as my heart beat fast. His rock-hard thigh was pressed against my leg, and a warm feeling ran through me as I clenched my legs. I wanted to move farther down the couch and away from him, but I didn't want him to realize how much he affected me.

"I came to give you your first test."

"Oh." I looked up at him then. "I didn't know you were a part of the tests."

"Why would you know?"

"Why did you choose me?" I burst out, unable to stop myself. "I feel out of place. All the other girls are so young."

"How old are you, Meg?"

"I'm twenty-five."

"You're young as well." He gave me a wry smile.

"The other girls all look like they're under twenty-one."

"Yes." He nodded.

"So why am I here?"

"I'm forty-two." His voice was humorous. "Many would say you're still too young for me."

"Forty-two?" I was surprised. He was older than I'd thought. Older than I'd thought I would be interested in.

"You sound surprised. Brandon is forty-two as well."

"What does that have to do with anything?" I blinked at him and watched as his expression changed.

"You didn't date him, did you?" His eyes narrowed as he surveyed me. "I was taken aback when I met you. You don't seem like his type."

"How rude." I glared at him, feeling rejected.

"Grew up with *Full House*, did you?"

"What?"

"How rude!" he said in a young, feminine, singsong voice and I laughed in surprise.

"I did watch it when I was younger. I guess I was channeling my inner Stephanie Tanner."

"I guess you were." He moved closer to me and I felt his arm slide around my back. "So if you didn't date Brandon, how do you know him?"

"Why do you care?" I swallowed hard as I felt his hands rest upon my shoulders, and his fingers started kneading into my muscles, massaging my balls of stress and tension.

"I don't really care," he murmured, and I felt his breath on the back of my neck.

"Why are you in here with me?" I jumped off of the couch. "What's the test?"

"You're eager, aren't you?"

"No. But I'm here for a job. Nothing else."

"Tell me about yourself, Meg."

"What?" I frowned back at him. "Is that the test?"

"Perhaps."

"What do you want to know? I was an attorney. I got fired. I applied for a job as a bartender and I ended up here. At this private club. And now I'm in training for a position I know nothing about."

"How does that make you feel?" He stood up, and I felt his arms on my waist turning me towards him.

"I don't know." I shrugged and looked up at him. "I don't know anything anymore."

"You're not the sort of girl we usually have coming through the doors."

"I suppose I'm not the sort of girl you hire, either."

"No, you're not." His eyes bored into mine seriously. "You're older than the girls we normally take in."

I glared at him. "Well, no need to spare my feelings."

"Brandon and I started this club in college." His voice was soft. "We were best friends and roommates, and I convinced him to start it with me."

"Why are you telling me this?"

"I'm not sure. Maybe so you'll trust me."

"Why do you want me to trust you? You don't even know me." I stared at him for a second and saw his expression go from light to hard again.

"Your assignment is to give me a lap dance." His tone changed and he sat back down on the couch.

"A lap dance?" My voice cracked. "Are you joking?"

"What were you expecting?" He leaned back in the chair. "A spelling bee?"

"I'm not giving you a lap dance." I shook my head.

"How badly do you want to know about Brandon's involvement with the club?"

"I don't care." Katie's face flashed in my mind and I sighed. "Why would you tell me if it's bad? Wouldn't that incriminate you as well?"

He chuckled. "Spoken like a lawyer."

"Don't you care?"

"Are you going to report me to the police?" He raised an eyebrow at me, and my breath caught. He looked like the devil incarnate as he sat there with his legs spread open and his arms stretched out. His eyes sparkled in the darkness of the room, and his face looked dark and ominous. Greyson Twining wasn't a man to play games with. I was positive of that fact.

"I have nothing to report to the police," I said and then gasped as his fingers grabbed my wrists. "What are you doing?"

"I don't want you to fail your first test."

"So this is a strip club? Or should I say 'a private strip club.'"

"Is that what you think it is?"

"Yes." I nodded and stepped towards him. I wanted to see the look in his eyes up close.

"And you're okay with taking a job as a stripper?"

"I'm a lawyer," I muttered defensively.

"So that means you're not okay working as a stripper?"

"I'm an unemployed lawyer." I fell against him as I lost my footing when his hands started caressing my ass. "What are you doing?"

"You work out, huh?"

"What are you talking about?" I muttered, shifting my footing to get away from him but somehow ending up closer to him.

"Your ass cheeks are tight." He laughed and squeezed. "I can feel your muscles clenching beneath my fingers."

"Get your hands off of my ass."

"Okay." And just like that, his fingers were gone. My fingers fell to his shoulders, and I grasped them as I stood up again. "So, Meg, tell me why you really came to get a job here."

"I told you. I need to make some money and I thought that bartending would be a way to earn a lot of money fast."

"Yet you have to know that this isn't just a bartending job. Why are you still here?"

"Why do you care?" I stood in front of him, looking down into his eyes. I was so close to him that I could see his chest rising beneath his shirt. If I reached my hands out, I could be touching his warmth against my palms.

"I care about everyone who works here, especially those who aren't here for the right reasons."

"Brandon Hastings is my best friend's boyfriend." I sighed. "Or ex-boyfriend, or whatever. I'm not really sure what they are right now."

"Oh." His voice sounded surprised, but he gave me a dazzling smile. "So you're telling me that Brandon wouldn't care if I fucked you?"

"I don't know why he would care."

"Interesting." He looked at me thoughtfully. "Then his phone call was more about me than you."

"So I guess you don't want to sleep with me, now that you know." I sounded disappointed, and I couldn't stop myself. I didn't know why I cared. It wasn't like I was going to sleep with him anyway.

"I never said that." His voice was a growl, and his arms grasped my waist and pulled me onto his lap. "In fact, I want to fuck you even more now."

"I said sleep with, not fuck," I whispered as I shifted on his lap. I could feel his hard erection beneath me and it felt like it was growing every time I moved. I enjoyed the feeling of him gently teasing me, and I made sure to keep up my soft movements in hopes of teasing him as well.

"I don't sleep, Meg. I only fuck." His voice was no-nonsense as he whispered in my ear. "I fuck hard and deep, and when I'm done, I'm gone."

"Romantic," I whispered into the air and he chuckled.

"I take it that doesn't impress you?"

"Who would that impress?" I tried to jump up, but his hands were firmly planted around my waist and he wasn't letting me go anywhere.

"Most women are happy when they hear how deep I can go."

"I'm not most women." A surge of jealousy ran through me as I thought about him with other women. *Get a grip, Meg. He's not yours.*

"I think I realize that." His lips nestled into my neck and he kissed me softly, gently biting the skin before licking it. "But I think you'd still be happy to feel how deep I can go."

"You're crude."

"No, I'm just honest. I thought women appreciated honesty."

"I do," I moaned as his teeth bit my neck harder. I wiggled in his lap, and his right hand used that as an excuse to grasp my right breast. "Greyson," I moaned, wanting him to stop but not wanting to say the words that might make him actually stop.

"Meg." He said my name with a throaty voice, and his fingers gently squeezed my nipple.

"Is this part of the training?" I mumbled after a few seconds. I was finding it very hard to speak coherently.

"No." His left hand reached up to my other breast now and he shifted underneath me. I felt his hardness between my legs, and I sighed as both of his hands fondled me. I closed my eyes to enjoy the feeling of excitement that had sprung up in my body. I ignored the voice yelling at me to get up and slap the living daylights out of him. It just felt so good.

The music changed then and I recognized the song as being one of Barry White's. I groaned as his deep voice filled the air, and unconsciously, my body started moving on his lap. My hips slowly started moving back and forth as I gyrated on his lap. I groaned every time I felt his cock rub against my pussy. Even though we were both wearing clothes, I could feel him just as well as if we were naked. My panties grew moist at the thought of rubbing up against him naked.

How would it feel to have his hardness up against me, teasing every fiber of me, pushing and tantalizing me, trying to gain entrance to me? I started moving back and forth on him even faster, guided by the smooth, sexy tones of the music and my own images. His fingers slipped under my shirt and traced their way up my stomach and to my bra. They were firm and soft at the same time and left a trail of fire on my skin as they deftly unclasped my bra. I gasped as I felt his fingers gently cup my breasts and then roll my naked nipples. The coolness of his touch against my fevered skin caused me to jump slightly, and I heard him groan behind me as I came down hard on his cock.

"What are you doing to me?" he groaned into my hair as his fingers continued to tease me. I ran my fingers along the side of his thighs and continued my movements, not wanting to think about anything other than this moment.

I then felt his right hand slide back down my stomach and stop right underneath my belly button, and my body stilled as I waited to see what he was going to do next. I didn't have to wait long.

His hand continued its descent and his fingers slid down the front of my pants until his hand was firmly wedged between my legs, and his fingers lightly rubbed me. I groaned then, a loud, unsatisfied lustful sound. I wanted to feel his fingers next to me. It wasn't enough to feel them lightly through my pants, not with the gentle strokes he was providing.

I increased my pace on his lap then, moving quickly and roughly against his cock and squeezing my legs together so that I could feel his fingers harder against me. He laughed softly behind me, and his hands moved to my waist again and turned me around so that I was straddling him.

"What?" I moaned and slowly opened my eyes to look at him. He was staring at me with a darkened gaze, his lips curled up and his eyes masked with some emotion I didn't know.

"So you're ready to give me my lap dance now?" He smiled at me then, a deep smile, and his eyes lit up as if they were laughing at some hilarious joke.

"What's so funny?" I mumbled, my body feeling bereft as clouds of doubt seeped into my brain.

"For someone so vocally against fucking and what I want to do to you, you certainly surprised me."

"I'm not against fucking." I leaned forward and bit his lower lip hard. "In fact, I quite enjoy fucking." I shifted in my lap so that I was sitting directly on his erection. "I just don't like being used."

"I'm not using you." He shook his head and his hands grasped my hips and started moving them back and forth. "In fact, I gave you a job."

"I don't even know what the job is."

"Do you really want to know?"

"I want to know if Brandon Hastings is bad news," I whispered into his ear while lightly nibbling on his earlobe.

"If I tell you that Brandon is bad news, you'll think I'm bad news as well."

"Well, aren't you?" I kissed down his neck and shivered as his hand pushed my butt hard against him. "But to answer your question, yes, if you tell me that Brandon is bad news, I will also assume that you are bad news."

"Well, I guess I should be honest." He chuckled, but there was no humor in his tone.

His hands ran up my back, and I leaned forward to kiss him. His lips tasted salty, and I kissed them eagerly, wanting to taste him again before he told me the truth. My tongue sought entry into his mouth and he sucked on it eagerly as I moved back and forth on his lap, building up the pressure in my pussy.

I knew that I should sit back and hear what he had to say, but I was scared. I wanted to experience this moment before he told me the truth and I had to leave. Because I would leave. I wasn't a masochist. At least that was what I tried to tell myself.

Greyson kissed me like a professional. His lips and teeth and tongue were all consuming. I couldn't think about anything but the pressure of his lips on mine and the sweet pleasure that ran through me as he sucked and nibbled on my tongue. He was so good that I didn't realize that he had successfully pulled my top and bra off until I felt my naked breasts pressed against his chest.

"Oh," I moaned against his lips as I felt his fingers kneading into my naked back and my nipples pressed against the soft cotton of his shirt. My fingers quickly reached for his buttons and opened his shirt up. I wanted to feel my skin against his skin. I wanted to feel the light spattering of his chest hair against my nipples, teasing them gently as his fingers kneaded into me roughly and his tongue explored my mouth.

"To answer your question, Meg," he muttered before bending his head down to my breasts. His eyes looked up at me and I stared at him wordlessly. "To answer your question, I would say if Brandon is bad news, then I am even worse news." His eyes were dark and his words were bold. I stared at him for a moment, about to ask him what he meant, but then his lips reached down and took my nipple in his mouth and I was taken on a new journey.

His teeth weren't gentle as they bit down on my nipple, and I cried out as he bit and sucked and then sucked and bit. My hands found their way to the top of his head and my fingers played with his silky tresses as I leaned back. His mouth changed from one breast to another, and as his teeth bit down on my other nipple, I felt a small orgasm building up in my body.

I groaned as he continued sucking and his fingers slid down my back and in between my ass. This time, he wasn't hesitant or gentle with his fingers. His hands slid roughly between my legs with the simple intent of rubbing me and bringing me pleasure as he suckled on my breasts. I moaned and my head fell back as his fingers found my spot and continued to rub me as his lips and teeth took possession of me.

The orgasm that had been building in me reached its peak and I felt my body trembling on top of him as I climaxed. I shifted uncomfortably in his lap, self-conscious about what had just happened, and I noticed that he was smiling at me.

"What?" I tried to wriggle off of his lap, but his hands remained firm on me.

"I didn't expect you to come." He laughed and his fingers moved up to play with my breasts.

"You were teasing me."

"Through your clothes."

"My breasts aren't covered."

"You didn't say no."

"I didn't complain." I shrugged, hoping he couldn't see my burning face. "I got mine."

"You sound like a guy."

"So?" I shifted in his lap again, trying to get off of him. His cock was still resting against my pussy, and all I wanted was to feel him inside of me. The orgasm I had experienced was only the beginning of the fireworks that my body wanted to experience.

"I want you." He kissed my lips. "I want to tear your pants off and I want you to ride me. I want you to ride me hard and fast and press your breasts in my face. I want to suck on your nipples as you bounce up and down on my hard cock and then I want to flip you over and fuck you from behind. I want to fuck you so hard that you'll be screaming my name out, begging me for mercy. And then I want you to get down on your knees and suck me off until I'm moments from coming. Then you'll get back on my lap and ride me slowly and we'll both experience the best orgasms of our lives."

I stared at him, unblinking and silent. My heart was racing with anticipation and my fingers were unconsciously gripping his arms. His words had turned me on and I waited patiently for him to undo my pants. I wasn't going to say no. I knew that I should say no, but I wasn't going to. I didn't want to. I wanted him badly. I had wanted him from the moment I had seen him.

A voice was screaming at me, but I couldn't move. I'd always been the responsible one, the wait-until-you're-in-a-relationship-and-in-love girl. But that had been boring, and it hadn't gotten me anywhere. I'd never had one night of unbridled passion. My pussy had never ached for a cock the way it was aching for Greyson's cock right now. I wanted to feel him inside of me. I wanted to feel how big he was, how deep he could go. I wanted to make him forget his own name. I wanted him to make me forget everything.

I waited patiently for his fingers to move to the top of my pants. I wasn't going to say no. I didn't care how bad he was. Not in this moment. Not when my body felt like this.

"Okay, you passed the test." Greyson's voice was soft, and I stared at him in confusion as he lifted me up and placed me on the couch next to him.

"Huh?" I mumbled, slightly dazed and very confused.

"While you technically didn't give me a lap dance, the way you moved your hips showed me that you could give a good one."

"But, I thought ..." I mumbled, angry at myself for feeling disappointed.

"You thought I was going to fuck you?" This time he was standing in front of me and looking down. His eyes looked hawkish and his body seemed overpowering as he stood in front of me, tall and strong.

"I, uh ..." I looked around for my bra, not wanting to sit there partially naked in front of him anymore.

"I told you that I won't fuck you until you beg me for it." His fingers reached down and traced a line from my cheek to my trembling lips.

"You're a—" I started, but he pushed his finger into my mouth to stop me from continuing.

"Shh." He shook his head. "Or it will be something much larger than my finger in your mouth."

"You wish." I pushed his finger out of my mouth.

"No, Meg. I think you do." He grabbed my hand and pulled it to the front of his pants. "You see what you did to me, Meg, with your teasing and grinding. I'm aching to be sucked off by you. But not until you're ready. Really ready."

"Whatever." I squeezed his cock gently and quickly unzipped his pants before slipping my fingers into his boxer shorts and grasping his cock in my fingers. I smiled to myself as I felt his sharp intake of breath. I allowed my fingers to run down the full length of his hard cock, and I shifted in my seat as I started feeling turned on again.

He was big, long, and thick, and I swallowed hard as I imagined him inside of me. I reached the tip of his cock and squeezed gently. He groaned again and I let my fingertips caress him as they grew wet with his pre-cum. I ran my fingers down to his balls and squeezed them a few times before allowing my nails to trace down him again. Then I removed my fingers from his pants and zipped him up again.

I stood up and stared at him. This time it was his eyes that were dazed, and I could hear that his breathing was now uneven.

"I guess it's time for my next test." I smiled at him sweetly while gently pressing my breasts against his chest. "Thanks for making this one so enjoyable." I gave him a quick kiss on the cheek and then grabbed my bra and put it on quickly.

"You're not what you seem, are you?" Greyson's voice was deep, and I could hear a hint of surprise.

"You're not the only one who's not transparent." I grabbed my shirt and pulled it on before walking quickly to the door. My heart was beating fast and my legs were trembling with fear. I was scared that he would come and stop me.

I knew that if he touched me again, it would be all over. I would be begging him. My panties were moist and my nipples were on high alert. My body was calling out for his touch. But I didn't want him to know. I wanted him to think that I couldn't care less. I wanted him to beg me.

"You don't want to play with me, Meg." His voice was soft. "And you don't want to doubt your gut instincts about me. What you first thought was correct. I'm not the sort of guy you want to play with. I know what I want and I take it. No questions and no regrets. I'm not the bad boy turned good. I'm just me. You don't want to forget that."

"I won't," I whispered back to him.

"If you're here to get answers for your friend Katie, then you're not going to be very lucky. If you want to be a good friend, I'd leave now. I'd leave while you still have your dignity intact."

I opened the door slowly and was about to walk out when I heard him speak again.

"I'd leave and I'd go and tell your friend to get as far away from Brandon Hastings as possible. Because yes, he's bad news. He's very bad news."

I walked out of the door and then ran to the bathroom. I walked quickly to the sinks and splashed water on my face. I smoothed my hands over my hair and took a deep breath. I stared at my reflection in the mirror and studied my face to see if

I looked different. I certainly felt different. My body felt more alive and my brain was buzzing with adrenaline. Then I heard a sound and froze.

"Hello?" I called out, and a door opened behind me.

"Meg?" Nancy's voice called out to me and she stepped out of a stall. Her eyes looked bloodshot, and I could tell she had been crying.

"Are you okay?" I walked over to her quickly, concerned.

"I'm fine." She nodded and rubbed her eyes. "It's hard being here."

"Did you find out anything?"

"No," she sighed. "Not really, though Frank said he recognized me."

"He did?"

"Well, he said I looked familiar. Asked if I had a sister or relative that used to work at the club."

"What did you say?"

"I pretended to be confused and said no." She bit her lower lip. "The way he looked at me, it made me shiver. He looked so menacing."

"Did Maria ever mention him before?" I asked thoughtfully. "Frank doesn't look that old. I doubt he would have been here when Maria was here."

"I don't know, but the look he gave me ..." She rubbed her eyes again. "I don't know if I can do this."

"You're strong." I grabbed her hands. "You want to know what happened to your sister, right?"

"Yeah." She nodded. "He asked me what room I was staying in, and he asked me who my roommate was."

"Frank did?" My eyes narrowed. "Why does he care?"

"I don't know. I told him." She looked at me with wide eyes. "I couldn't think of a reason to not tell him. What if he comes to our room tonight?"

"He won't."

"He asked me about you."

"About me? Why?"

"I don't know." She shook her head. "A lot of people have been talking about you."

"Why?"

"I, uh, I ..." She blushed and looked away from me.

"What is it, Nancy? Tell me?"

"You're older than the other girls." She shrugged. "I guess everyone is just surprised."

"I'm only twenty-five." I'd never felt so old before in my life.

"I know." She shrugged. "I guess it's just unusual."

"I guess," I sighed. "I wonder what really goes on at this club. I'm so confused."

"Yeah, I wonder if it's a prostitution ring." Nancy gave me a look. "Like a whorehouse."

"Whorehouse?" This time it was my eyes that widened. "I thought it was a strip club or something." I paused and thought for a moment. "Though, I guess the next logical step would be a whorehouse." I felt a headache looming. Was Greyson in charge of a whorehouse? I felt saddened as I thought about it. Was I just another whore to him? And what did that mean about Brandon? Was he also in charge of a whorehouse? Was Katie dating a pimp?

"We better go." Nancy sighed and pulled out some lipstick. "I think it's time for the next room."

"What was your first test?"

"I had to do a spelling test." Nancy made a face and I stared at her in shock.

"What?" I asked her with an open mouth.

"I had a spelling test. I think I failed. I'd never even heard of half of the words."

"Are you joking?" I burst out laughing. Was this some sort of big joke?

"Not at all." She made a face. "That's why I was crying. I'm worried I may not make it through the training period. I know I failed that test."

"I thought you were crying because of Frank."

"Oh, no. He creeps me out, but I knew coming into this that there would be plenty of creeps to deal with."

"Oh?"

"Well, Greyson Twining is the owner." Nancy shrugged.

"You know him?" I asked lightly.

"Maria told me some things when she first started," Nancy whispered. "I was young so didn't really understand then. But sometimes I remember things that she said."

"What did she say?"

"He's a bad guy." She looked at me with a worried expression.

"In what ways?" I questioned her.

"We have to go." She shook her hair. "We'll talk later."

"Okay." I tried not to sigh. Every time I felt like I was going to get some information from Nancy, she disappeared. I was certain that she knew a lot more than she was letting on, and I didn't understand why she wasn't being more forthcoming. Especially since I had said I would help her.

CHAPTER FOUR

I walked to the second room for my second test deep in thought. I was so caught up in thinking about my conversation with Nancy that I almost missed Elizabeth whispering in the corner of the hallway with Frank. I slowed my pace and cocked my ears up, hoping to hear what they were talking so fervently about.

"I don't know if I can do this," she whispered. "I'm not that kind of girl."

"You knew what you were getting into." Frank's voice was rough, and I saw his hand slide around her waist. "If you're a good girl, I'll—"

"Take your hands off of me!" she hissed and stepped back.

"You know you want it." He leered at her, and I stood there wondering if I should go and say something. "Don't try and deny it."

"I'd rather have Greyson."

"I thought you wanted Hastings."

"Well, the bigger fish is Greyson." She laughed. "I've heard he knows how to work what he has."

"Don't you go fucking this up." He looked angry.

"Oh, shut up, Frank. Don't worry. I can fuck and work."

"Slut." His hand fell to her ass and squeezed. "Just get what we need."

"It'll be like taking candy from a baby." She pressed herself into his chest, and I gasped when she leaned forward to start kissing him. This was not what it seemed at all.

"He wants us to shut her up if she tries to—" Franks eyes spotted me then and he quickly pushed Elizabeth away from him. "Can I help you?"

"Just looking for my next test room." I smiled wide, trying to pretend I hadn't just heard their conversation. "I swear I get turned around so easily. You know us blondes."

Frank looked at me with narrowed eyes and Elizabeth glared at me. "I guess I need to try the next corridor." I giggled and ran my hands through my hair. "I guess you can tell it's not dyed."

"Yeah, we can." Elizabeth's tone was catty. "No one would ever dye their hair that shade on purpose."

"Oh, you never know," I replied back with a wide smile. "I mean, look at the shade you chose."

I turned around quickly and walked back down the hallway with a small smile on my face. Elizabeth was such a bitch, but I knew I shouldn't have said anything. She could be a wealth of information to me; it looked as if she knew a lot more about the club than I did.

And she seemed to know Frank—shady, acne-ridden Frank. He still gave me the creeps, but I had a feeling that he knew exactly what was going on here and what had gone on before as well. It was a pity that neither of them would be allies. If anything, they were both in deep. I just wished I knew exactly what they were involved in.

I waited a few minutes and then went back up the hallway to enter the next room. This time I was in a bedroom. It reminded me of some sort of French boudoir, with its tall, stately bed and white shimmery nets hanging from the side. The duvet was plush and ivory, and there was an ivory-colored vanity next to the wall.

I looked around the room for a pad or notebook to see what my next test was going to be. I couldn't see anything, and my heart beat fast as I wondered if Greyson was going to join me in the room. Not that I wanted him to. I needed to clear my mind out. I needed to think. There were so many pieces to this puzzle, but none of them were making sense.

"Walk to the vanity," a voice spoke in the room, but I couldn't see where the speakers were this time. "Walk to the vanity and open the drawer. That is where you will find your next test."

I walked over to the vanity slowly, slightly disappointed. I sat on the bench and opened the drawer. Inside the drawer was a single piece of paper. I pulled it out and read quickly.

The paper said, *The night is day, the day is night, do you think you can stay up with no light?*

I turned the paper over to see if there was any more information on the other side of the page. It was blank. I turned it back to the front again to reread what it had said. But there was nothing I had missed.

I looked inside the desk to see if there was another note I had missed. There was nothing else there.

I looked around the room. The bed looked so inviting and I yawned just staring at it. I'd had a restless night the evening before, and it would be so refreshing if I could just sleep for about twenty minutes.

I was about to jump up and walk over to sit on the bed when I dropped the paper in my hand. As I bent down to pick up the paper, I noticed that there was something sticking out from under the leg of the vanity. I frowned as I leaned over and pulled out the small piece of paper.

It was tiny and had been screwed up. I unscrewed it carefully and looked at it eagerly, wondering if this was the real test. There was a little note on the paper, and I read it quickly, my heart beating fast as I realized what it said. *"Trust no one. I thought he loved me. Fail the tests. It's the only way out. Maria."* I stared at the paper for a second and then put it in my pocket so I could show Nancy.

Wasn't her sister's name, Maria? And now that I thought about it, hadn't Katie said that Brandon's college girlfriend was called Maria? And wasn't his new fiancée called Maria as well?

My head spun, and I wished I were able to call her and ask. Where were all these Marias coming from? Was there a connection?

I closed my eyes and tried to remember all the details I knew about the Marias. But then the lights went out and I froze.

I made my way to the mattress and sat down on the bed. It was soft and plush, and I decided that it wouldn't hurt if I lay back on the bed. The pillow was soft underneath my head, and I closed my eyes and snuggled into the sheets. I was starting to get a headache. I was confused and upset. Nothing was making sense, and yet I knew I couldn't leave. Not now. Not when my mind and body were a jumble of nerves and questions.

"Meg?" His voice was deep, and I shivered as I looked towards the open door.

"Yes."

"Hey." He walked towards the bed and he sat at the edge.

"What do you want?" I sounded hostile and I was glad.

"I came to see how you were doing."

"Oh?"

"This test is about staying awake."

"Staying awake?"

"Because of all the late nights we have here at the club." Greyson chuckled.

"I see."

"I'm not being serious. It's about staying alert."

"Why are you telling me that?"

"Because I don't want you to fail."

"Sure."

"Can I lie down next to you?"

"Don't you have anything else to do?"

"I wanted to talk to you."

"Why?"

"Because you interest me."

"What about me interests you? My breasts?" I was being sarcastic and I didn't care. I was annoyed at how excited I felt inside now that that he had joined me in the room.

"I'd be lying if I said that your breasts weren't as sweet as they were juicy," he drawled, and I felt a tingling in my stomach.

"So this test is just about me staying awake?"

"In so many words." He lay back and rested his head on the pillow next to mine. "How are you liking it here, Meg?"

"It's fine."

"What about your roommate? Her name is Nancy, right?" he spoke casually, but my heart stopped beating.

"Yeah, she's fine too."

"She seems a little wide-eyed and bushy-tailed," he continued. "Almost too wide-eyed and innocent."

"I don't know what you mean," I said breathlessly as I felt his thigh resting against mine.

"I don't know. I get the feeling she has an agenda."

"I wouldn't have a clue."

"Things aren't always as they seem, Meg." His voice was low. "Sometimes, the wolf is the wolf and sometimes he isn't."

I changed the subject. "So, you went to college with Brandon, right?"

"Yeah, we were at Harvard together. It seems like a million years ago now."

"So you knew Maria?"

"Maria?" He repeated her name sharply.

"Yeah, Maria. His college girlfriend."

"Brandon didn't have a girlfriend in college named Maria."

"Maybe she was his fiancée?"

"Brandon didn't have a fiancée in college named Maria." He rolled over to face me. "Where did you hear that?"

"Nowhere. I must have gotten confused." I ran my hands down his chest. "What was Brandon's fiancée's name?"

"You're obsessed with him." His fingers grabbed ahold of mine. "Let's not talk about him."

"Have you ever been engaged?" I closed my eyes and listened to the sound of our heartbeats echoing in the room as our fingers played with each other.

"Me?" His voice sounded dry. "No. I've never been engaged."

"Oh, wow. Why not?"

"Never been interested in going down that road."

"Never?" I opened my eyes and turned towards him.

"I'm not the sort of guy that gets married."

"Why not?"

"I'm just not. What about you? Ever been married or engaged?"

"No." I paused. "How old are you again?"

"Forty-two."

"Forty-two." My voice rose as I remembered. "I thought once men hit their forties, they wanted to get married."

"You know a lot of men in their forties?"

"No." I stared into his eyes and smiled. "I don't."

"You're not missing anything."

"I never thought I was."

"Just some of the best sex of your life."

"What?" My eyes widened and he laughed.

"When you're with a man like me, women start to wonder why they ever dated younger."

"I thought younger men had more energy. They can keep it up longer."

"You've obviously never been with an older man."

"And you've obviously been with lots of younger women who have given you a big head."

"I don't date younger women."

"You mean you only sleep with them?"

"No." His lips curled up and his fingers traced my jawline. "I try to stay away from women who are under thirty."

"Oh?" I was disappointed. "Why?"

"Too much drama. Too many dreams. Too much hope."

"You prefer them old and jaded."

"Thirty isn't old." He laughed. "Only someone in her twenties would say that."

"So you prefer women in their thirties then?"

"No," he chuckled, and his fingers fell to my neck and then collarbone. "Thirties, forties, fifties … It's all the same to me."

"You would date a woman in her fifties?" I couldn't keep the shock out of my voice.

"I'm forty-two, Meg. Fifty isn't that much older than me. Much like men, women only get better as they age."

"I don't believe you would date a woman in her fifties." I shook my head and then stilled as his fingers found my breasts and gently kneaded them. "An older woman wouldn't put up with your crap."

"What crap?" He leaned in closer to me and whispered against my lips. "Older women actually prefer my honesty and my lovemaking skills."

"I don't care," I muttered, closing my eyes to ignore the jealous feelings filling me up. I didn't want to think about him with older women. I felt stupid that I was getting jealous. I didn't know him. He could do what he wanted with whom he wanted. "Let me guess, you would also date someone in her eighties. I imagine a woman that age would have every skill you could think of. Maybe she even invented some of the positions we talk about today."

"There's no need to be catty, Meg. Weren't you just complaining about ageism earlier today?"

"Whatever," I moaned, and my eyes flew open as I felt his lips on mine, kissing me softly.

His tongue entered my mouth and I sucked on it gently. I'd show him that just because I was in my twenties, it didn't mean that I didn't have a few tricks up my sleeve. I'd show him that I could give just as good as I got. My hands flew to his hair and then to his back as we kissed. I wrapped my legs around his waist and he groaned against me.

"You don't act like a woman who doesn't want to be kissed and touched." He pulled away from me and quickly pulled my top off. "In fact, you seem like you quite enjoy it."

"Whatever." I pulled his shirt off as he unclasped my bra.

"You have beautiful breasts." His fingers gingerly played with my nipples.

"Am I supposed to say thank you?"

"You can." He laughed and gave me another surprised look. "You're different than I thought you would be."

"Because you're the expert on women?"

"I know women pretty well. I knew when I saw you yesterday in your slutty outfit that you weren't a slut."

"Really?" It was my turn to laugh. "I sure feel like a bit of a slut right now."

"Why?" He grinned at me before dropping his mouth down to my right breast and sucking gently on my nipple. I squirmed beneath him as his fingers continued playing with my other nipple. I couldn't believe that I was letting him do this to me, but my body couldn't resist.

"Because you could be the shadiest man alive and I'm … oooh!" I cried out as he teeth bit down hard on my nipple and then sucked gently. "Oh, God, Greyson!" I cried out again as he continued his assault on my nipples.

"Yes, Meg?" He looked up at me and winked.

"Nothing," I groaned. "Absolutely nothing."

"If they could see you right now …"

"Who?" I whispered, confused.

"All the people who thought you were a goody two-shoes."

"What people?"

"The people who would be shocked to see you making love to a man you met yesterday."

"We're not making love."

"I'm sucking on your nipple and I'm about to devour you with my tongue. It's as close as we can get without my cock filling you up."

I pushed against him reluctantly, not really wanting him to stop what he was doing but not wanting him to think I was succumbing this easily. "You should go. I have to pass this test."

"I think I'm helping you pass." He kissed down my stomach. "I've a feeling you would have fallen asleep if I hadn't joined you."

"Maybe, maybe not."

"This way, I can guarantee you will stay awake."

"You're so cocky."

"I'd rather have my cock in."

"Funny." I rolled my eyes and he laughed.

"What can I say? You bring out my inner comedian. The one that hasn't been seen in a long time."

"You wanted to be a comedian?"

"Yeah, actually. When I was in high school." His tongue entered my belly button and he kissed my stomach. My legs clenched together as my panties grew wet.

"Really?" I knew I sounded surprised.

"Yes, really." His voice sounded nostalgic. "When I was in elementary school, one of my uncles took me to a stand-up show. I thought it was hilarious and practiced every night for about five years. Then, when I was a sophomore in high school, I put on a show. The crowds loved me. Everyone loved me and thought I was hilarious. I then decided that I was going to be a comedian when I grew up, but my father eventually persuaded me otherwise."

"Oh?"

"Enough about me." He continued kissing my stomach and then I felt his fingers undoing my pants. I froze as he slid my pants down my legs and onto the ground. "Let's focus on you."

"Do you wish you had become a comedian?" I pressed on, wanting to know more about the real Greyson as I had a feeling this was a side of him that very few people got to see.

"No." His voice was gruff and his fingers roughly pulled my panties down. "Now be quiet."

"Don't tell me what to—ooooh." I fell back against the bed and cried out as he buried his face between my legs. "Greyson!" I gasped as his tongue licked around my clit furiously. I could feel his breath on me and I shivered, but my pussy was aching to feel his tongue on my aching spot. "Please." I clenched my legs around his neck and shoulders, trying to force him to lick me on that spot with his tongue. He continued to circle my clit, and I reached down and grabbed his shoulders, squeezing them hard and pushing him closer towards me. "Please," I pleaded and then cried out in pleasure as his tongue finally touched that spot. His mouth closed in on my clit and sucked hard. "Oooh!" I screamed as my body trembled and buckled beneath his touch.

As soon as his tongue entered me, I came. I couldn't control it, and I felt him lapping up my juices eagerly as I climaxed on his face. I lay back after my orgasm was finished, feeling both satisfied and hornier than ever. But Greyson wasn't done. Instead, I felt his fingers spreading my legs wider and his tongue back on me.

"Again?" I whispered as my body shivered at the light touch of his tongue teasing me again.

"I could do this all day. You taste so sweet and salty," he groaned against me and kissed back up to my face. "Taste yourself on me."

"No." I shook my head.

"I want you to taste what I taste." His lips pressed against mine and his tongue entered my mouth slowly. I trembled as I lightly sucked his tongue. My hands were in his hair and his fingers were tracing lines around my breasts when I felt the tip of his cock next to my stomach.

"What are you doing?" I gasped as I reached down and felt his bare cock hanging out of his pants.

"What are you doing?" he whispered back as I continued caressing his cock. He pulled away from me slightly, placed the tip of his cock on my clit, and started rubbing it gently against me.

"No," I groaned as my body buckled underneath him. The feel of his hardness on me was too much for me to take, and I could feel another orgasm building up.

"You don't like it?" His cock continued teasing me, and I felt the tip of him at my entrance. My whole body stilled as I waited for him to enter me. "Answer me, Meg." He looked down at me with lust-filled eyes. The tip of his cock moved about a centimeter inside of me and I wriggled on the bed to get him to fill me up completely.

"I like it," I whispered and reached my arms around his back to push him into me. "Please."

"Please what?" He laughed and slowly withdrew the tip of his cock so that it was rubbing up and down on me again, tormenting me with pleasure. It felt long and hard and ready, and I wanted to reach down and grab it and push it inside of me.

"Nothing." I wrapped my legs around his waist, but my strength was nothing compared to his.

He chuckled as he rolled onto his side.

"Greyson," I moaned as I felt him put his cock back into his pants.

"Yes, Meg?" He leaned into me and whispered in my ear. "Is there something you want?"

"No." I kissed his neck and bit down on him hard. I heard him laughing as I gave him a hickey.

"No need to take your frustrations out on my neck."

"I'm not frustrated," I lied and lay back.

"Sure," he teased, and the room grew silent as we just lay there cuddled into each other. His fingers lightly played with my breasts, and my fingers ran up and down his chest. I felt comfortable curled up next to him, and I felt my eyes growing droopy.

"Don't fall asleep, Meg," he whispered against my hair.

"I just need a quick catnap."

"No." He pinched my bottom and then laughed when I yelped. "No catnaps."

"So what shall we do?" I whispered, hoping he would change his mind and make love to me without me having to beg.

"Let's talk." His hands ran down my back. "What's your favorite TV show?"

I sighed as I realized that no lovemaking was about to happen.

A part of me wanted to question him further about Brandon's Maria and Nancy's Maria, but I knew it would be foolish of me to ask anything else without having more information. I also felt guilty. Like I was playing both sides. Only I didn't really know either side.

Part of my brain was screaming at me and calling me a fool. I was starting to fall for this handsome stranger I didn't know. A man who had told me himself that he was bad news. Greyson Twining was a man with warning signs flashing all over him, only I was ignoring every single one of them.

***

"Are you going to join me in each room?" I asked him as we exited the room. "Going to make sure that I pass every test?"

"No." He shook his head. "I don't know if I can stop myself if I come into another room with you. My cock is dying to burst out of my pants and actually enter you the whole way. I don't think I could stop myself if I came into another room."

"I think you have better self-control than that."

"You sound like you want me to join you in every room." His eyes looked at me solemnly. "Don't go getting soft on me, Meg. I'm not a wolf in sheep's clothing."

"You confuse me." I shook my head. "I don't get why I'm here or what you want from me."

"I started this club, Meg. I started this club because I wanted power. I wanted to rule the world. I wanted all my needs satisfied whenever I wanted." His voice was bleak. "Don't go thinking this is anything more than it is."

"I'm not." I turned away from him, hurt. I'd thought we were finally getting to know each other. "I couldn't care less about you."

"I don't think that's true." His eyes looked at me with a closed expression. "And that's why I'm warning you."

"Warning me about what?"

"Everything." He shrugged. "I have to go." He gave me a deep, soulful look before leaning down and slowly kissing me. His lips tasted of sex, and I melted against him, kissing him back passionately.

I didn't want this, whatever it was, to stop. My body was buzzing with sexual excitement and nerves. I was a bundle of a million different emotions. I didn't know what was going to happen, and I didn't care. All I wanted was for this feeling to continue. No matter what happened at the end, it would be worth it.

***

I walked into the third room with bated breath. Even though Greyson had said that he wasn't going to join me in the room, I was still excited. I was growing to like Greyson, even if I didn't really know or understand him. There was something about his honesty that was both refreshing and nerve-racking. I'd already gone further with him than I had expected I would go. But I didn't regret it. Not for a second.

Being at the private club made me feel like I was finally living and finally doing something important. I'd gone into law because I had wanted to make a difference in people's lives, but all my job had really consisted of was reading lots of cases and documents and writing lots of briefs. And I wasn't helping anyone but big corporations get out of their tax liabilities. My job had paid well, but I had always felt a little depressed at the firm. I'd always felt like I was wasting my talents and my life.

I knew that Katie thought I'd loved my job, and I hadn't wanted her to feel sorry for me, but a part of me had been glad to be fired. Even though I had no clue as to why. Even the human resources department had been surprised when they had laid me off. In fact, I thought I'd seen a few tears in Maggie's eyes as she'd realized that I wasn't going to fight for some answers. I thought she'd thought they'd broken me. But the reality of it was that I hadn't cared enough. I was scared and fearful about money, but I also knew that this was a new start for me. I wanted a new life.

I looked around the third room curiously, wondering what my third test would be and also looking for the most comfortable place to have sex. Because, in my mind, I was already picturing Greyson and me on the floor.

I figured that I might even be able to plead with him to make a phone call. I really needed to talk to Katie and find out more about Brandon and Maria. I could have sworn that Maria had been Brandon's girlfriend in college. I'd remembered Katie crying in jealousy over the fact. So either Brandon had been lying or Greyson was now. And that made me suspicious. Why lie about something like that? It made no sense.

This room was different from the other two. It looked like an office, and there were plenty of folders and notepads spread around the various desks. I shivered as I pictured myself bent over the grand mahogany table with Greyson behind me. I'd have to grip the edges of the table hard to keep my balance.

I walked towards the table excitedly. I'd always had a fantasy of doing it in an office since I'd watched the movie *Secretary*. There was something so primal about doing it in a place of work—it was both sexy and scintillating.

I shook my head as I saw the note on the desk with my third test. "Priorities, Meg," I lectured myself as I picked up the note.

This was a fairly mundane task. All I had to do was file all the folders on the desk and put them in a filing cabinet. I wasn't sure how this was a helpful skill for a stripper, but I supposed it wasn't for me to wonder. After all, I didn't really know what this club was about. It was the best-kept secret on the planet.

I picked up the first files and had a quick peek inside to see if Maria or anyone else had left any clues inside. I was about to open the filing cabinet when I heard the door open and the light went off. My heart started pounding. I'd known he couldn't resist me. Greyson had come to take me.

I stood there, waiting patiently, unable to see a thing as the room was pitch black. I realized that he was waiting for me to go to him, so I walked slowly in the area of the door.

"You came," I whispered as I walked across the room. I could hear him breathing, and a shiver of lust ran down my spine.

He didn't respond, so I continued towards him. My hand touched him first and he pulled me towards him. His fingers clasped my waist tightly and my breasts crushed into his chest. I ran my fingers down his chest, and his hand reached up and pulled my hair. I moaned as I felt his lips crushing down on mine, and his fingers roughly squeezed my ass.

It was then that two things happened that filled me with shock. I breathed in his smell and realized that something was off. It didn't smell like Greyson. And then I heard his voice.

"Brandon, it's Greyson. You need to get down here. There's a new girl and she's asking questions. We may have a problem."

I froze as I realized that Greyson was out in the hallway. That meant he wasn't in the room with me. That meant that I wasn't kissing and being kissed by him. That meant that the man whose paws were all over me wasn't Greyson.

I pulled away quickly and was about to scream when a hand flew to my mouth.

"I advise you to keep quiet, Meg." His voice was deep, and I swallowed hard.

He'd just confirmed something else to me. This wasn't a case of mistaken identity. Whoever was with me had known I was going to be in this room. The man I was with knew exactly who I was and I had absolutely no idea who he was.

AUTHOR'S NOTE

Thank you for reading *The Private Club* series. If you enjoyed the series, please leave a review.

There will be a follow-up series called *The Love Trials* starting in April 2014 that will focus on Nancy and the other secrets at *The Private Club*.

There is also a sequel coming out called *After The Ex Games* that provides insight into Brandon, Katie, Greyson, and Meg's lives. *After The Ex Games* and *The Private Club* Serials.

Please join my mailing list to be notified as soon as new books are released and to receive teasers: http://jscooperauthor.com/mail-list. You can find links and information about all my books here: http://jscooperauthor.com/books. I also love to interact with readers on my Facebook page: https://www.facebook.com/J.S.Cooperauthor.

As always, I love to here from new and old fans, please feel free to email me at any time at jscooperauthor@gmail.com.

ABOUT THE AUTHOR

J. S. Cooper was born in London, England and moved to Florida her last year of high school. After completing law school at the University of Iowa (from the sunshine to cold) she moved to Los Angeles to work for a Literacy non profit as an Americorp Vista. She then moved to New York to study the History of Education at Columbia University and took a job at a workers rights non profit upon graduation.

She enjoys long walks on the beach (or short), hot musicians, dogs, reading (duh) and lots of drama filled TV Shows.

Made in the USA
San Bernardino, CA
19 October 2014